JEAN DE BRUNHOFF

BABAR
AND HIS CHILDREN

Translated from the French by Merle Haas
Random House   New York

Other books in this series

This title was originally cataloged by the Library of Congress as follows:

Brunhoff, Jean de,   Babar and his children.
Trans. from the French by Merle Haas.
Random House ©1938
unp. col. illus.   1 Picture books for children   I. Haas, Merle, trans.   II. Title   E
ISBN: 0-394-80577-1   0-394-90577-6 (lib. bdg.)

One morning Babar said to Cornelius: "Old Friend, you who have been my constant companion through good times and bad, listen now to my wonderful news. Celeste, my wife, has just told me that she is expecting a baby."

Then, pointing to the footstool, he continued: "Here is a new hat for you and also a message I have just written to my subjects. Take it and read it to all the inhabitants of Celesteville."

After having congratulated and thanked Babar, Cornelius puts on his full-dress uniform. Standing before the gateway of the Royal Palace, he tells his drummer to assemble the townspeople.

4

Slowly he unfurls the King's proclamation, puts on his spectacles, and reads in a loud voice. The elephants, gathered together in large numbers, listen respectfully.

B

Dear and Loyal Subjects

When you hear a salute fired from a cannon, do not be alarmed. It will not mean that another war has begun, but simply that a little baby has been born to your King and Queen in the Royal Palace.

In this way you will all learn the glorious tidings at the same time.

Long live the future Mother, your Queen Celeste!

Babar

Here, reproduced exactly, is Babar's message, which Cornelius read.

Babar is trying to read, but finds it difficult to concentrate; his thoughts are elsewhere. He tries to write, but again his thoughts wander. He is thinking of his wife and the little baby soon to be born. Will it be handsome and strong? Oh, how hard it is to wait for one's heart's desire!

Celeste urges him to go for a ride on his bicycle, to take his mind off the big event, and Babar finally consents.

After having pedalled several miles, he finds a pleasant spot and decides to rest. Seated on the grass, he admires the surrounding countryside, Celesteville and Fort Saint John. "It is from there that the cannon will be fired," he says to himself.

At this very moment: **Boom!** Babar hears the salute. "There it goes! What a shame that I wasn't at home!" thinks Babar. He immediately mounts his bicycle and rides home as fast as he can pedal.

There, up on the turret, the Artillery Captain of the King's Guard carries out the orders he has just received by telephone. He gives the command. One blank shot is fired, then another and finally a third.

The elephants gather in groups on the promenade and begin to wonder and ask questions. King Babar had only mentioned one shot. Why did the gunners fire off three? Cornelius himself cannot understand it.

Babar reaches home quite breathless from his fast ride. He also had heard three shots. He dashes headlong up the stairs, joyfully rushes into Celeste's bedchamber and embraces his wife tenderly.

She smiles and proudly shows him three little baby elephants. That explains everything. One salute for each child; three babies=three salutes. But what a surprise to find three babies when you only expected one!

The Old Lady has one in her arms, and the nurse holds the other two. Arthur and Zephir are terribly excited. Babar has given them permission to come and see the babies. They walk in quietly. "Oh! How tiny!" says Zephir. "Oh! How cute!" adds Arthur, as he admires the baby lying in the cradle.

Celeste had prepared only one cradle; so the nurse quickly makes another one out of a wash basket, a towel and an umbrella. It is crude, but the babies are warm and sheltered.

Here are the babies, settled now in the garden and asleep
in a big perambulator. Babar and Celeste receive the congratulations
of their friends. Almost everyone brings a gift.

Poutifour, the farmer, and his wife bring fruits from their own orchard; the hens offer some eggs; the gardener some flowers. The bakers present a huge cake, and Cornelius brings three silver rattles.

Now Babar and Celeste have to find three names for their children. Of course they had discussed this beforehand. Pom, Pat or Peter? Julius, John or Jim? Alexander? Emil? Baptiste? Alexander isn't bad, but what if it's a girl? Juliet, Virginia or . . .

"We'll simply have to come to a decision about their names," says Celeste to Babar. "I'd like our daughter to be named Flora."

"I'd like that too," says Babar, "and as for the two boys, I think we might choose Pom and Alexander."

After having repeated Pom, Flora and Alexander in one voice, Babar and Celeste declare: "That's perfect. Let's keep these names."

Every week Dr. Capoulosse puts the babies in his big scale and weighs them. One day he says to Celeste: "Your Majesty, the babies aren't gaining fast enough any more. You must supplement their feeding with six bottles of cow's milk, to which you must add a table-spoonful of honey."

The little ones soon get used to the bottles. Arthur and Zephir like to watch them drink. Pom is the greediest and the fattest. He is the one on Celeste's lap. He always cries when his bottle is empty.

1 Flora is very good
and lies in her cradle
playing with the rattle
which Cornelius gave her.

2 She throws it up in the air
with her trunk.
What a nice jingly noise
it makes!

3 She puts it
in her mouth and
sucks it.
What fun!

4 Suddenly,
she doesn't quite
know how,
she swallows it.

She chokes,
gets purple in the face,
and her trunk trembles.
Celeste rushes to her.

She grabs her, turns her
upside down and shakes
her. But still the rattle
won't fall out.

Fortunately
Zephir manages to
pull it out
with his hand.

Flora is saved, but
she cries most bitterly.
Her mother tries
to comfort her.

Now the children begin to run about and play in their big sunny nursery. Babar often comes in to play with them. Today he sits Pom on the end of his trunk and bounces him up and down. It's like our game "Ride a Cock Horse."

Cornelius hangs the ropes of a swing from the end of each tusk and Arthur gently rocks Alexander back and forth. The boys have learned to walk before their sister. Flora will soon follow their example. She can stand up alone already.

When the children are dressed, the nurse takes them out for a ride in their big carriage. They are still too young to walk very far. One day Nurse says to Arthur: "It is colder than I thought and we are not far from the house. It won't take me long to run back and get some sweaters so my babies won't catch cold. Will you look after them for me until I come back?" Arthur is very glad to be trusted and proudly pushes the carriage.

He pushes it twenty feet forward, then twenty feet back, and takes good care to avoid the stones. All of a sudden he hears the soldiers parading. As he turns around to watch them, he lets go of the pram. The path is slightly down-grade at this point, and the carriage begins to roll off by it-self. Pom, Flora and Alexander think this is very funny and laugh, but Arthur is frightened and runs after them. The grade gets steeper and steeper.

The carriage rolls faster and faster. Now the children are scared too. Arthur runs after it as fast as he can. Nurse comes back with the sweaters. Very much worried, she joins the chase. It looks as though the babies are in grave danger. Just a bit farther on there is a bend in the road with a deep ravine on one side. The carriage must be stopped before the bend or it will go straight on down into the ravine, and then . . . The accident! Martha, the turtle, out for a stroll, has seen it all coming and understands the situation thoroughly.

She hurries along on her short legs. Just as the carriage is about to topple over the precipice, she succeeds in throwing herself under the wheels! Suddenly checked while going full tilt, the carriage stops and almost turns over. Pom and Flora are jolted back against the hood, which saves them, but poor Alexander is thrown out head first. Nurse screams and the rabbit runs away.

Mr. and Mrs. Squirrel
have heard the
nurse's scream.
Then, a minute later,
they hear the
rustle of leaves
and the noise of
breaking branches to
the left above them.
They both look up
and see the head of
a baby elephant.
He is yelling for his mother in a frightened lisp.
"Mama! Alessander's falling! Mama! Help Alessander!"

"Steady, little elephant! Don't let go! We're coming!" cry the squirrels. "Just balance yourself and try to get your foot up on that big branch. We're right here. Don't be afraid. We'll help you!"

Their scheme succeeds. Mr. Squirrel gives further orders. "Hold fast to my tail and wiggle your big ears to keep your balance! Watch your step! Follow me! You can rest when you've reached our shelter!" A few minutes later, safe and sound in the squirrels' hole,

Alexander breathes a sigh of relief. How lucky he was to have fallen in the trees, and to have found these obliging friends! He might have been badly hurt! Now he'd like to go and tell his Mama not to worry. But how can he get down that tree trunk? It is absolutely smooth and very high! Just then a big giraffe strolls by and sees his plight. He says: "Look here, little elephant, I'll put my head right close to the branch.

Then you can sit down between my ears and hold on to my horns. I know your parents and I'll take you back to them."

Alexander, quite delighted, says good-by to the squirrels and thanks them. He settles himself on the giraffe's head, and off they go. Although the giraffe walks slowly, Alexander decides that he prefers his perambulator.

Informed by the nurse, Babar and Celeste are already on their way to the scene of the accident. What joy to be re-united! Arthur is ever so pleased.

A few months later, Babar decides it would be fun to go on a picnic. The weather is fine, and the family is in high spirits. Cornelius feels the heat, but joins them enthusiastically. Later, tired and hungry, they all sit down to a delicious lunch.

After the meal Celeste tidies things up. Babar goes off to fish in a nearby stream. Cornelius lies down in the shade to have a nap. Alexander mischievously wriggles under Cornelius' derby hat and walks about with short steps. "That's a funny-looking tortoise!" says Pom.

While playing, they come to the edge of the river. Alexander has another bright idea. He puts the hat in the water. "Nice boat!" says he,
as he steps in to try it. "It floats! Isn't that marvelous?"

Just then the current catches the hat, and it drifts away from the bank. Alexander is enchanted with his boat ride, but Pom and Flora are a bit worried.

How can they get the hat back to shore? Flora begins to cry. She runs off to call her Mama, who was just beginning to wonder where the children could be. Pom runs along the bank calling: "Alexander, come back! Please, nice little ducks, oh, please bring my brother back!"

But the ducks fly away. Suddenly, Pom gives a lusty yell: "A crocodile! A crocodile!"

Alexander looks around. "Oh! Papa!" he whimpers.

Babar was peacefully fishing and thought the children were playing. As he hears this desperate cry for help, he understands that something serious must have happened. He stands up and trumpets angrily as he sees the horrible crocodile.

Three seconds in which to act—and no gun! The situation seems hopeless! Babar, without hesitating a moment, grabs the anchor and hurls it violently into the monster's jaws. Caught like a fish, the crocodile in a wild fit of rage flips his tail right out of the water. Tossed about by the swirling eddy, the hat capsizes and Alexander is thrown into the river.

Babar dives in after him, and searches about with his trunk. Ah! He feels something! Hurrah! It's Alexander's ear! He makes quick work of bringing him up out of the water and reviving him. As for the crocodile, he thrashes madly about, but cannot rid himself of either the anchor or the boat.

The birds gather around Babar and Alexander who are of course dripping wet.

"Would you be kind enough," asks Babar, "to go and reassure Queen Celeste? Ask her to hurry back to the house to lay out some dry clothes and prepare hot drinks for us. And you, dear little ducklings," he adds, "would you be kind enough to dive down and bring back my crown and Cornelius' hat? They are down at the bottom of the river."

Alexander kisses his Mama happily. She bathes him, gives him a good rubdown and puts him to bed under heavy blankets.

Arthur, Zephir, Pom and Flora are still very excited. The big flamingo brings back the crown and the hat. "Oh, thank you very much," says Babar. "The hat is slightly damp and out of shape. Cornelius, however, will be happy to have it back because it is an old keepsake."

Now everyone is asleep. Babar and Celeste will soon go to bed too. They are gradually calming down after all these exciting events.

"Truly it is not easy to bring up a family," sighs Babar. "But how nice the babies are! I wouldn't know how to get along without them any more."